This book was entirely drawn and painted using writing ink and slow-dry blending medium.

First published in South Korea as 지난 여름 (*Last Summer*) by Woongjin Thinkbig Co. Ltd., Seoul in 2017
First published in English by Floris Books, Edinburgh in 2021. First published in the USA in 2022. Second printing 2022
© 2017 김지현 (Kim Jihyun). English version © 2021 Floris Books. English translation rights arranged by S.B. Rights Agency
– Stephanie Barrouillet on behalf of Woongjin Thinkbig Co. Ltd. All rights reserved. No part of this publication may be
reproduced without the prior permission of Floris Books, Edinburgh. www.florisbooks.co.uk
British Library CIP data available. ISBN 978-178250-742-0. Printed in China by Leo Paper Products Ltd

Floris Books supports sustainable forest management
by printing this book on materials made from wood that
comes from responsible sources and reclaimed material

MIX
Paper from
responsible sources
FSC® C020056

The Depth of the Lake and the Height of the Sky

Kim Jihyun

Floris Books

Last summer,
I stayed for a few days
in a lakeside town in another country,
surrounded by a thick forest of trees.
Soft sunlight warmed my skin,
a gentle breeze rippled across the deep lake,
countless stars sparkled high in the night sky.
These quiet moments I spent immersed in nature
made me feel truly alive.
To share that serene feeling,
I created this book.

About Kim Jihyun

Kim Jihyun (김지현) is an illustrator, graphic designer and picture book creator from South Korea. She studied Design and Illustration at the University of Brighton, UK, and Seoul National University, South Korea, and lives in Seoul with her husband and their young daughter. *The Depth of the Lake and the Height of the Sky* is Jihyun's first picture book. It was illustrated using writing ink, which allows Jihyun to express subtle emotions and to illustrate different qualities of light. The story was inspired by her feeling of serenity in nature; a stark contrast to her life in a busy city.